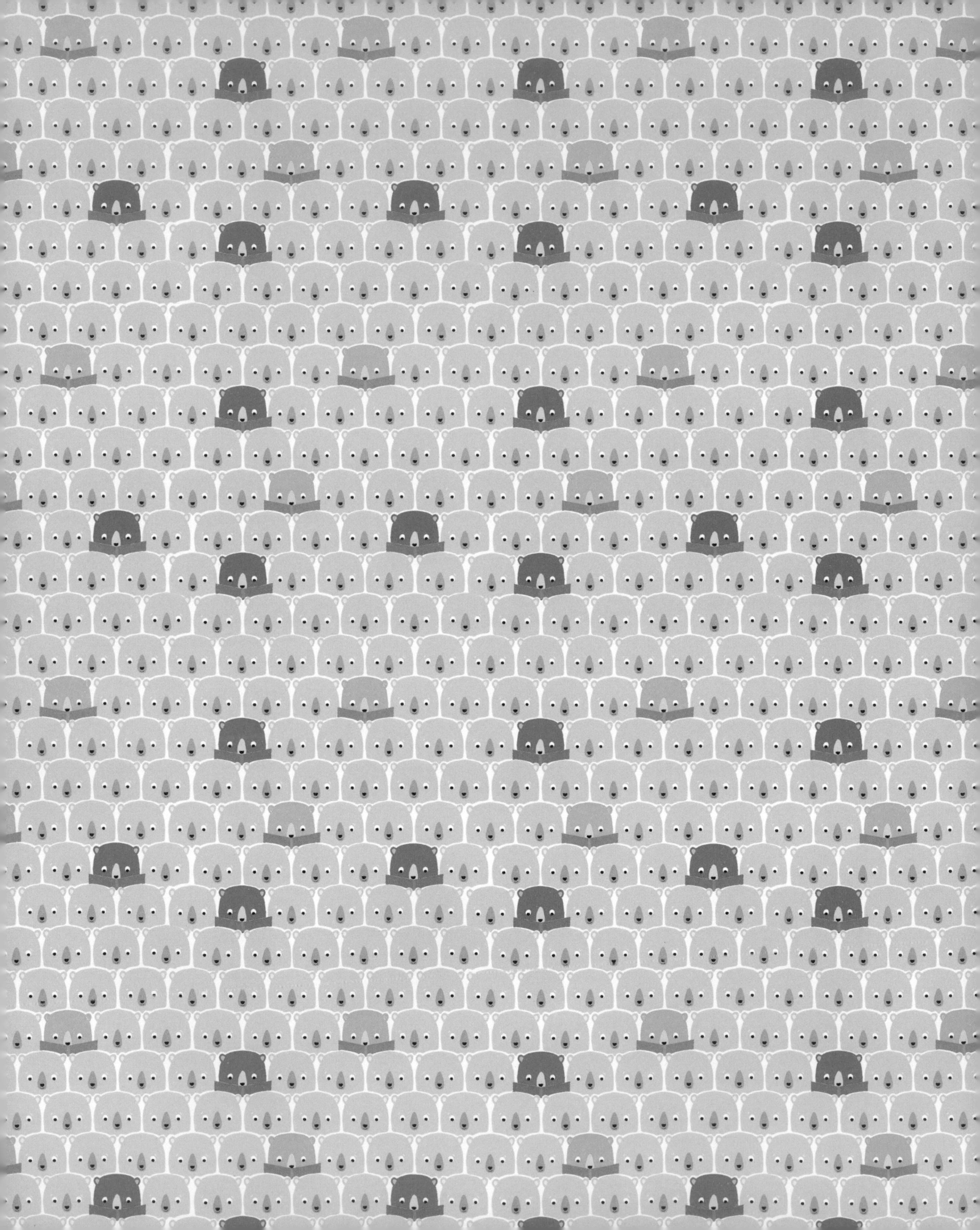

Bears Make the Best READING BUDDIES

written by Carmen Oliver

illustrated by Jean Claude

CAPSTONE YOUNG READERS
a capstone imprint

Published by Capstone Young Readers,
a Capstone Imprint
1710 Roe Crest Drive
North Mankato, Minnesota 56003
www.mycapstone.com

Text copyright © 2016 by Carmen Oliver
Illustrations copyright © 2016 by Capstone Young Readers

Library of Congress Cataloging-in-Publication data is available
on the Library of Congress website.

Summary: Adelaide doesn't want an assigned reading buddy.
She has her own, and he is perfect. She just has to persuade
her teacher to let her reading buddy stay, even if he is a bear.

ISBN: 978-1-62370-654-8 (hardcover)
ISBN: 978-1-4795-9181-7 (library binding)
ISBN: 978-1-4795-9182-4 (eBook)

Design Element: Shutterstock: Ursa Major

Designer: Aruna Rangarajan

Printed in China.
009205S16

For Caldwell Heights Elementary, continue to read and soar!
And for Cassidy, Halle, and Wyatt — the best
reading buddies a mom could ask for!
- Carmen

To Skye, Calum, Sam, and Fin — keep reading, buddies!
- J.C.

At the beginning of the school year,
Mrs. Fitz-Pea assigned reading buddies,
but Adelaide didn't need one.
She already had her own!

"Don't be scared,"
Adelaide coaxed.
"Come in."

"Wait!" Adelaide said.
"Bears make the best
reading buddies,
and I'll tell you why."

"Bears know how to sniff out a good book with their super-powered snouts.

They're wild about adventures . . .

and mysteries . . .

and fairy tales."

"They know how to build peaceful places where no one bothers you while you read.

They sit side by side, knee to knee, and put the book between you, so you both can see."

"Bears listen with their super-sensitive ears while you sound out the words.

And if you get frustrated, they wrap you up in warm bear hugs."

"Oh! And their claws are perfect page-flipping tools . . .

...most of the time."

rrriiip!

"But don't worry! They always carry a spare jar of honey for making repairs."

Quick Object Anemone Thermometer Rabbit

"Bears know you never run away
from hard-to-pronounce words.
They challenge you to look at
the pictures and chew over
the possibilities.

Anemone Thermometer Perplex Quant
Rabbit lonely farther

And when you get it right . . ."

"... they stand on their hind legs
and roar so you'll keep going."

"Finally, when you come to the end
of your book, bears are always hungry
for more — especially books about
salmon fishing and berry picking."

"Bears know that once you get a taste for books, you'll discover trail after trail of adventure and clamber to new heights."

"And that is why bears make the very best reading buddies," Adelaide finished.

"Well, don't just stand there, Adelaide," said Mrs. Fitz-Pea. "Show that bear in!"

"I'll read to you," Adelaide said.
"Then you can read to me."

And when Adelaide started to read,
Bear burrowed in and got lost in the story.